Princess Cupcake Jones

and the
Missing Tutu

By Ylleya Fields

Illustrated by Michael LaDuca

Belle Publishing
Cleveland, Ohio

Dedicated to my children, especially my daughters, who are absolutely my inspiration.
To my parents, the Kohls & JDE, without them this project
never would have seen the light of day.♥
Special thanks to K.T, M.L. and L.W.

Belle Publishing
5247 Wilson Mills Rd #324
Cleveland OH 44143
www.BellePublishing.net

Book design and illustrations by Michael LaDuca, Luminus Media

---

Publisher's Cataloging-In-Publication Data
(Prepared by The Donohue Group, Inc.)

Fields, Ylleya.
  Princess Cupcake Jones and the missing tutu / Ylleya Fields ; illustrated by Michael LaDuca.
    p. : col. ill. ; cm. -- ([Princess Cupcake Jones series])

  Summary: Follow Cupcake Jones in the first book of her series as she searches the royal castle for her beloved tutu, and learns the importance of cleaning up.
  Interest age level: 003-008.
  ISBN: 978-0-578-11303-6

  1. Princesses--Juvenile fiction. 2. Tutus (Ballet skirts)--Juvenile fiction. 3. Orderliness--Juvenile fiction. 4. House cleaning--Juvenile fiction. 5. Princesses--Fiction. 6. Tutus (Ballet skirts)--Fiction. 7. Orderliness--Fiction. 8. House cleaning--Fiction. 9. Stories in rhyme. I. LaDuca, Michael. II. Title. III. Title: Cupcake Jones and the missing tutu

PZ7.F545 Pri 2013
[Fic]

In a rose-covered palace at 6 Garden Place,
sweet Cupcake Jones won't wear velvet and lace.
Although she's a princess, as everyone knows,
she flounces her tutu wherever she goes.

3

Creeping through gardens, finding new bugs.

Cartwheeling over the soft palace rugs.

Painting a picture, watching the moon,

or riding her pony on a warm afternoon.

Cupcake listened to Mommy's soft voice as she read,
and dreamed of wearing her tutu to bed.
But Mommy said, "No" (and Mommy knew best),
so each night she gave her tutu a rest.

One morning, awakened right after dawn,
the princess exclaimed, "My tutu is GONE!"

"Was it stolen by robbers? Where did it go?"
She lined up her dollies all in a row.
"Have you seen my tutu? Oh, please, please say yes!"
But the dollies were quiet. They just couldn't guess.

Cupcake ran up to Mommy, a frown on her face.
"My tutu has vanished without any trace!
Was it taken by fairies who crept in my room?
Or snatched by a witch who flew off on her broom?"

The Queen smiled at Cupcake. She shook her head, no.
"Now, come along Princess, it's soon time to go.
An artist is painting a portrait of you!
Since your tutu is gone, this pink dress will do."

"I don't want that dress. It just isn't me! If I hurry I'll find my tutu, you'll see!"

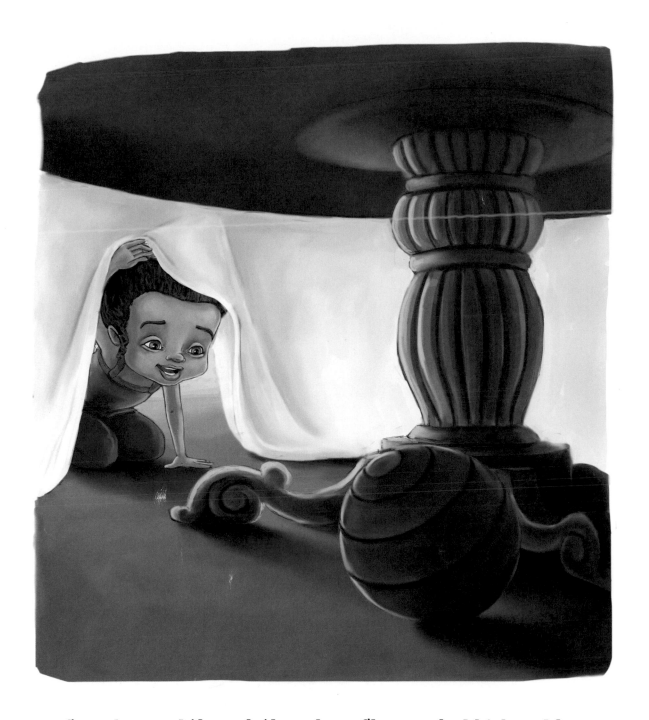

Cupcake raced through the palace. She searched high and low,
and found favorite things that were lost long ago.
Right under the table inside the main hall,
the princess discovered her missing red ball.

In the big, palace kitchen bustling with cooks,
she found her amazing magic trick books.

In Daddy's office where the king spent his day,
she climbed up his shelves and found her beret.

"I see something pink!" Cupcake flew down the stairs.
But instead of her tutu, she found her pink bears.

The washer was empty. No tutu in there.
"I can't find it, Mommy, I've searched everywhere!"

"All of your toys were here all along
but left in a place where they didn't belong.
When you put things away, I promise you then,
what's special to you, won't be missing again."

20

Cupcake leaped up and ran through her room.
"Could it be here?" She picked up a broom.
"Will I find my tutu if I clean up this mess?
'Cuz I don't want to wear that silly old dress!"

Cupcake hurried and tidied her fairytale books

and put her collection of hats on their hooks.

She danced and she skipped and she twirled and she hopped,
while she polished and dusted, straightened and mopped.

As she cleaned up her room, it was ever more clear, what
Cupcake thought lost, was always right here:

a boa,

some lip gloss,

a miniature zoo,

an earring,

a jump rope,

and one ballet shoe.

She counted her bracelets. She hung up her clothes.
"I won't lose you again." She kissed her bear's nose.

The tea party cups, she stacked high on their tray.
At last, Cupcake's things were all put away.

The princess then slid across the sparkling, clean floor.
"Yippee! My toys won't be lost anymore!"
Then Cupcake stopped. What was not there?
"WHERE IS MY TUTU?" she cried in despair.

Throwing herself on her big fluffy bed,
she suddenly noticed what hung overhead.
A rainbow of colors—orange, yellow and blue.
She looked up in wonder...could it be true?

Hooked on the fan, where she tossed it last night...
"MY TUTU! MY TUTU!" she shrieked with delight.

Hearing the noise, the Queen rushed through the door,
where the princess was twirling across the clean floor.
"I found your tutu! I knew that you would!"

you

"I put things away, Mommy, just like I should.
I'll hang my tutu each night on its hook,
so when I wake up I'll know where to look!"

With her tutu on, Cupcake skipped on her way,
to have her portrait painted that day.